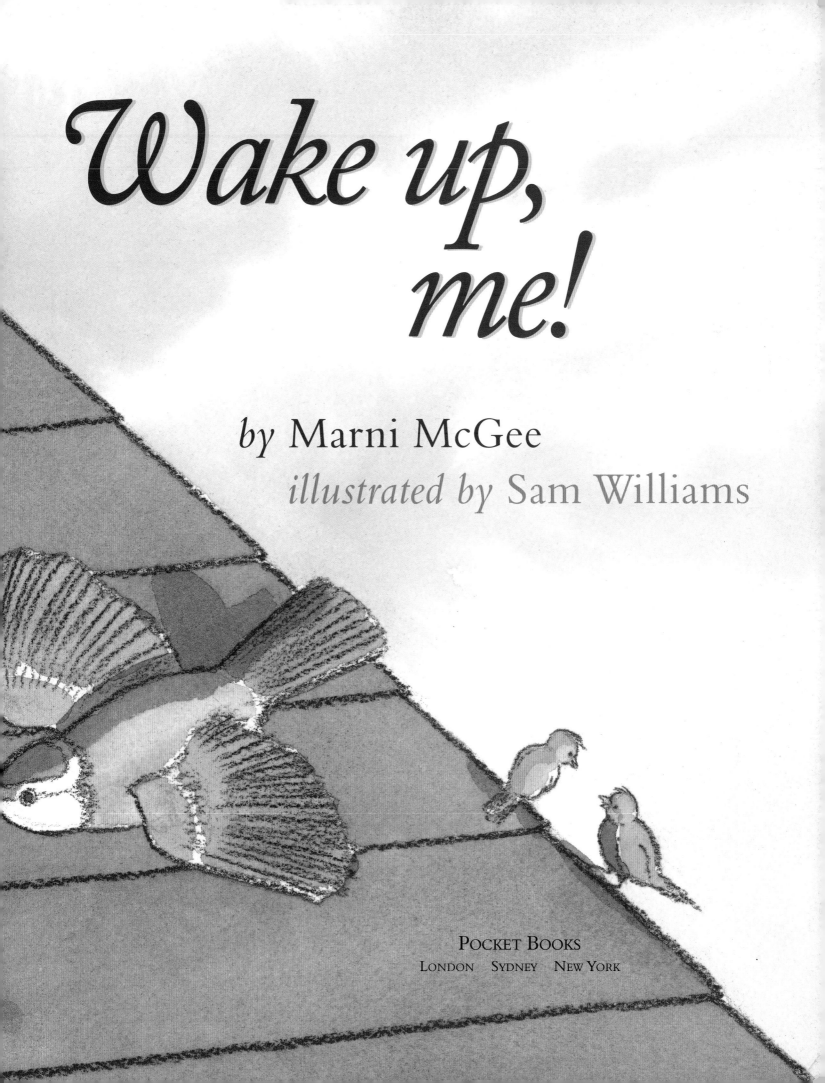

Wake up, me!

by Marni McGee

illustrated by Sam Williams

POCKET BOOKS

LONDON SYDNEY NEW YORK

POCKET
BOOKS

First published in Great Britain in 2004 by Pocket Books,
An imprint of Simon & Schuster UK Ltd
Africa House, 64-78 Kingsway, London WC2B 6AH

Originally published in 2002 by Simon and Schuster Books for Young Readers,
an imprint of Simon & Schuster Children's Publishing Division, New York

Text copyright © 2002 Marni McGee
Illustrations copyright © 2002 Sam Williams

Book designed by Jennifer Reyes and Mark Siegel
The text for this book is set in Aldine Bold
The illustrations are rendered in watercolours

A CIP catalogue record for this book is available from the British Library upon request

ISBN 0-734-9008-8

Printed in China

1 3 5 7 9 10 8 6 4 2

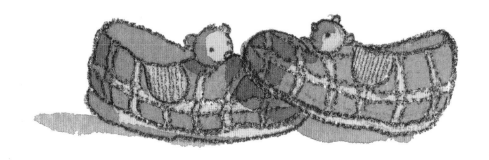

In loving memory of my grandfather, Dr Thomas Benton Sellers, and in honour of my mother, Katharine Sellers Broach — a woman of unselfish love and abundant joy

— M. M.

To my children . . . for all those wonderful moments

— S. W.

Wake up, ears.
Wake up, eyes.

No more lazy,
sleepy sighs.

Wake up, nose. Wake up, chin.

Here comes giggle.
Here comes grin!

Wake up, birds.
Wake up, breeze.

Blow on
flowers . . .

tickle trees!

Wake up, legs.

Wake up, feet.

Tummy says it's time to eat.

Wake up, spoon.
Wake up, plate.

Mummy . . .

look how much I ate!

Wake up,
coat.

Wake up, cap.

Tie my shoes
on Daddy's lap.

Wake up, door.

Wake up, day.

Bear and I are set to play.

Wake up,

wake up, me!